THE ALIEN CONSPIRACY

AN UNOFFICIAL FORTNITE NOVEL

BATTLE ROYALE: SECRETS OF THE ISLAND BOOK TWO

THE ALIEN CONSPIRACY

AN UNOFFICIAL FORTNITE NOVEL

CARA J. STEVENS

Sky Pony Press
New York

Sky Pony Press books may be purchased in bulk at special discounts for
sales promotion, corporate gifts, fund-raising, or educational purposes.
Special editions can also be created to specifications. For details, contact
the Special Sales Department, Sky Pony Press, 307 West 36th Street,
11th Floor, New York, NY 10018 or info@skyhorsepublishing.com.

Sky Pony® is a registered trademark of Skyhorse Publishing, Inc.®,
a Delaware corporation.

Visit our website at www.skyponypress.com.

10 9 8 7 6 5 4 3 2 1

Library of Congress Cataloging-in-Publication Data is available on file.

Cover design by Brian Peterson
Cover artwork by Alan Brown

Print ISBN: 978-1-5107-4434-9
E-book ISBN: 978-1-5107-4435-6

Printed in Canada

TABLE OF CONTENTS

CHAPTER ONE: JIN

Freefall was the most exciting part of training. It had twice the excitement and none of the danger of actually falling to the ground at 200 kilometers an hour. Even though I knew it was my avatar hurtling toward the ground, I heard the rushing air and felt the wind whipping around my face and hair. I scanned the island below, which looked just like the map from up above, and located my target—Haunted Hills. I adjusted my direction and out of the corner of my eye saw Asha, Zane, and Jax do the same, as if we were playing a silent game of follow-the-leader.

This was my first launch as squad leader, and I was surprised to find I was not too nervous. I mean, the stakes weren't that high. It was a playground training session, not a Battle Royale, but still, I was responsible for picking the landing spot and calling the shots. When we were almost in position over Haunted Hills, I pressed the button to deploy my glider. The wind stopped rushing. A calm silence took its place. I had nothing to do but float down and enjoy the ride. This was my favorite part of training. It was the only quiet time I had to myself to think, prepare, and look at the scenery.

The ground came up beneath my feet too quickly. We all hit the ground running in the northern part of the sector. In all our trips down to the island, this was our first time in Haunted Hills, although I had studied the maps and video replays late into the night to prepare for this moment.

My communicator crackled to life, and Zane's cheerful voice came through loud and clear. "Where to, squad leader?" He was speaking his native Australian English, but his words came through in perfect Korean thanks to the universal translator lodged in my ear. I wasn't sure if Asha heard his words come through in English or Swahili, as both were spoken in her native country of Kenya, and Jax had told me he heard everything loud and clear in English spoken with a Chicago accent.

"Let's check these stone buildings and chapels. I heard there may be some good loot chests out in the open here, but stay low. I saw another squad land just south of us," I warned them. I slinked around the area, keeping my guard up and my eyes open. In the relative quiet of the moment, I had a chance to look around, noticing the low stone monuments that looked like memorials to former residents. If there were any ghosts or mysteries lurking on the island, I got the feeling they'd be here.

"Payday!" Jax called out.

"Did you say Mayday?" Asha called. "Where are you? Do you need help?"

"Your com is acting up again, Asha. He said 'payday'," I clarified, worrying that Asha's com might be malfunctioning again. "And what does *payday* mean, exactly, Jax?"

"It means I found a chest. Now get over here and collect this loot before the big guy with the mech suit and the scary pickaxe comes back," Jax shouted.

I ran up the side of a nearby gravestone and vaulted to the top of a low chapel roof and crouched down, scanning the area for the cadet Jax mentioned. There was no sign of Jax's scary pickaxe guy, but I saw Jax just below me and another squad headed toward Haunted Hills in the distance. I jumped down and landed next to Jax, who looked up, startled.

"Where did you come from?" I pointed up behind me and Jax shook his head. "I'll never get used to your catlike pouncing and sneaking up on people. I'm just glad you're on my side, or you could have sniped me ten times over by now."

I laughed. "I'll take that as a compliment." I looked at the glowing cache of weapons scattered around and gave Jax first choice, then picked up something lightweight and short range for myself. Haunted Hills was a crowded little place, so a long-range sniper wouldn't be of much use. "What did big pickaxe guy look like? Strange he should be traveling alone so early in the drop."

Jax shook his head. "I didn't get a good look at him. I only saw him from behind. He was wearing a mech suit. As soon as I landed, he threw down a bouncer and took off."

Asha came running over and stopped right in front of me without a word. "What's up, Asha?" In response, she shrugged and tapped her communicator. Her com had gone out again. That suit was more glitchy than a fake highlight reel. I reached out and fiddled with a loose wire at the top of her avatar's headset where the signal dish was mounted. There was a loud crackling sound, then Asha's voice came through midsentence. ". . . think that might have been the problem. Oh! It's back! Hello!" She smiled cheerfully and leaned in for a hug. "Thank you for the patch, Jin." An avatar hug is a strange thing—you don't feel it exactly, but you know it's happening.

Asha picked up a weapon and a small chug jug. "You guys mind if I drink this?" We both shook our heads, and she drank it down, activating a shield.

"I'll pop out and see if we have company," she said and then took off around the corner.

"There's a squad headed this way from the east," I told her, then searched my map. "Have you guys seen Zane?"

"I'm all right," Zane called out. "Found a nice quiet chapel with a fair bit of loot inside. Picked up some bandages and a big fat chug jug, too." We heard drinking sounds through the com. "Shields up!" he called out.

Jax stood up and peered out over the gravestone cautiously. "Anyone else see that big mean guy I was talking about before?" I shook my head. "I'm going to head for higher ground, if that's okay," Jax asked me. I nodded and watched him run off like a snake, weaving his way around the gravestones for cover. I liked being the leader for once. I felt the responsibility for my squad mates, but there was also a great feeling of freedom.

Grateful this was just a playground exercise, I decided to throw caution to the wind and explore. I headed to the nearby chapel where I found Zane hacking at the floor. "Found another chest," he announced when he saw me. I nodded and headed upstairs. The building itself was fairly normal. I peeked out a window and saw the other squad inching closer. It looked almost like they were stalking something. Off to the left, Jax was chopping down a tree for supplies. The fallen tree caught the attention of the approaching squad, and they opened fire on him. He ducked for cover, and I aimed my weapon out the window, regretting that I had chosen the short-range one. Fortunately, Jax hadn't been hit. He popped up and shot back, scattering the squad. I recognized one of them as she ran closer to the church. It was Blaze, our former squad mate we had unanimously voted out when we had to pare our team down to four members.

I hoped she wasn't holding a grudge. "We have company," I announced over the com. "Blaze's squad is here, and it seems like their fire is not friendly. Zane, she's headed toward the church. If you aren't prepared for battle, I'd recommend taking the western exit."

"Gotcha loud and clear, squad leader!" Zane called out, then crashed through the western wall of the building and ran southward. I quickly smashed all the furniture I could find, collected the materials, broke through the upper wall, and threw down an exit ramp. I tucked and rolled down the ramp, did a cat leap, and landed on the ground. One of Blaze's teammates was running toward me with her weapon drawn. "Looks like they're using this playground session to sharpen their stalking skills," I warned my squad. "Too bad for them. Take evasive maneuvers. Remember, our mission today is exploration and strategy. Hold your fire unless it's for defense," I reminded them.

I did a dash vault over a nearby gravestone and ran to meet up with the rest of the squad to the south, just as we had planned. That was when I saw him, the big guy Jax had seen when we landed. From the back, his hulking mass was bigger than any of the other avatars, and he was carrying a scary looking pickaxe I had never seen in the registry. I thought I knew every cadet in the program, but I had never seen this suit before. I crouched low behind a bush and tried my best to stay invisible, but something must have caught his attention. He turned to look straight at me as if he knew exactly where I was hiding. I held my breath and tried to see his face through the leaves, but something was wrong. Either it was a trick of the light or the leaf cover was too thick, but I could have sworn there was no face looking out at me from behind the helmet. I saw a flash of pink, but before I could look closer, something else caught his attention off to the side, and he bounded off after it, leaving me shaken and confused.

I heard sniper shots through my com. "Everyone okay?" I asked.

"Yep. Just fired a warning shot to keep Blaze's teammate off my tail," Jax announced. They would be wise to steer clear of Jax. He was a sharpshooter with a sniper.

I checked the map readout and located my squad mates. They were all nearby in Haunted Hills, but not so close together that we'd run the risk of getting eliminated at the same time again. That's the kind of mistake a team only makes once. Especially since when it happened to us the first time, it led to public humiliation in front of all the cadets in the program. I trotted over to Jax's location atop one of the hills to the south. I told myself it was so I could get a good idea of the landscape from above, but really, I wanted to talk about the strange cadet we had both seen.

I could see the tower Jax was building well before I caught up with him. He was a clumsy builder, putting ramps where he should have used walls and wasting materials by building out. It wasn't an efficient sniper tower at all, but I wasn't there to judge him. This was a practice round, after all. "What's up?" I asked as I came alongside him. "Need any help?"

"Nah. Just practicing my builds," he replied, not missing a beat. "It's not my strong suit, but it's nice to build instead of destroy for a change."

His response surprised me. It was rare to get an opinion out of Jax. He usually just stuck to the facts. None of us knew much about him, other than what we had overheard the day we arrived. That if he hadn't come to HQ to join the battle training, he would have gone to jail or a juvenile detention center. That was enough to scare the rest of us from asking too many questions. But after living with him and watching him for a few months, he didn't seem all that scary. He mostly kept to himself, which is why I wasn't expecting to get much out of him on the subject of the strange visitor we had both seen.

"Any sign of the big guy with the pickaxe again?" I asked. Jax just shook his head and kept building. I stepped back and looked at what he had created. It wasn't a sniper tower after all. It was actually a house, and a pretty nice one at that. "What are you building?" I asked.

He stopped and looked at me before throwing down a floor and four walls. "Haven't you ever seen a house before?"

I felt my cheeks redden back at command center and hoped my avatar wasn't blushing as well. I should have expected a snide comeback. "Looks good," I stammered. "It's a shame it will disappear as soon as we leave." It really was shaping up to be a nice house.

"Don't you have somewhere to be?" he snapped, then took a deep breath. "Sorry. Forgot this was a team exercise. We don't get any time to ourselves in this place, and it's starting to get to me."

"I know how you feel," I replied. As a boarding school kid, I was used to being around people day and night, and most of the time, it was pretty awesome. But even I needed to get away sometimes, which is why I started doing parkour. Being able to climb up unreachable rooftops gave me the escape I always needed back home. Here in the HQ bunker under the endless sand dunes, the only rooftops were down on the island, and they all went away once the storm closed in. "Take your time and meet up with us down in Pleasant Park when you're done. Looks like the storm eye won't be closing in for a while today."

"If you guys are done with your coffee break, I think we should head down to the next stop on our island tour," Zane's voice broke in. I had forgotten face-to-face chats were broadcast to the whole group. We didn't have any secrets from each other in our squad, for better or for worse.

"I hear you, Zane, but sometimes it's nice to take advantage of playground mode to get in a little me time. Let's all meet up at the main church when you guys are ready," I replied.

I ran down the hill and speed-vaulted over the gravestones, reaching the chapel in record time. It was great using an avatar for parkour. I wasn't out of breath but still felt the thrill of overcoming obstacles and clearing my head as I ran. I had located and cleared out all the loot in the chapel while Zane and Asha were still making their way over, so I climbed to the roof and looked out across the landscape. Two moving figures caught my eye. I vaulted down to get a closer look. It was Blaze's teammate—a girl who looked like an office-worker-turned-spy—and she was running away from the mysterious player in the mech suit. He was in hot pursuit, and the girl kept tripping over obstacles as she ran. He was closing in on her so quickly that she didn't have time to draw her weapon. She threw a grenade behind her to slow him down, but he leaped over it, avoiding the explosion without breaking his stride. As he got closer, he didn't draw a weapon. Instead, he jumped into the air and pounced on her, knocking her avatar to the ground. A drone appeared overhead almost immediately. The mysterious player looked up, shielding his face from the light, then disappeared into the forest.

I waited for the girl's avatar to parachute back down after her suit reset. I scanned the skies but didn't see any sign of her. Could it be her suit had been damaged so much she couldn't come back from a playground elimination? I didn't wait to find out. I ran back to the chapel and waited for the rest of the team. Zane, Asha, and I arrived at the same time, and we sat down in the main room to regroup. We hadn't been there long when Jax sauntered in and sat near us without a word. I nodded to him and then addressed the squad. "Did anyone see the drone beam that girl up?" I asked. They all nodded. "Did anyone see her parachute back down?" They looked at each other and then back to me. They hadn't seen her either.

"She probably took the opportunity to explore another part of the island," Zane suggested.

I shook my head. "Blaze would never stand for that. She likes her team to stick together in close formation," I reminded them. She was a stickler for the rule book, even when it got her and her squad in trouble. I was glad she wasn't on our squad anymore, even if that did mean she was now our mortal enemy on and off the battlefield. "I think that mysterious pickaxe guy damaged that recruit's suit. That's why we didn't see it come down." I paused and decided to share what I thought I saw, no matter how strange it seemed. After all, we shouldn't be keeping secrets from each other. "I don't think that guy is a cadet. I got a look at his face and . . . and . . . well, there wasn't anything there. Just a pink blob . . ."

There was a pause, then the three of them burst into laughter. I guess telling them wasn't the right call after all.

CHAPTER TWO: ZANE

We all had a good laugh at Jin's expense. A blob for a face? That was funny. Everyone's eyes played tricks on them sometimes, but Jin was always ready to believe the unusual explanations over the rational ones.

"So, who do you think it was, really?" I asked, opening the floor to other theories. I hoped that Jin might take the opportunity to come up with another, less-wacky interpretation.

"I haven't seen the guy, but maybe someone's trying out a new avatar," Asha suggested.

"Or it could be Velasco experimenting with new training obstacles. Or a new way to keep an eye on us," I offered.

"I don't think it had a face," Jin said. I fought the urge to start laughing again, but Jin was deadly serious. He really thought he saw some kind of inhuman being.

"Maybe it was a mutant," Jax chimed in from the corner. I had forgotten Jax had seen him, too.

I wondered if he knew about the mutant theory or if it was just a guess. "What makes you think that?" I asked cautiously.

Jax shrugged. "He seemed big. And strong. He had faster reflexes than any cadet, and he pounced on that girl with all his strength instead of using his weapon."

Jax had a point, but I wasn't ready to talk about what I knew. Or at least what my parents had suspected and shared with me. "Well, let's leave Haunted Hills and branch out a bit today. Anyone know what the storm eye forecast is for today? When does it start shrinking?"

"We have about an hour left," Jin replied. "Let's go to Pleasant Park as planned and goof around a bit. We've more than earned a little playtime. What do you guys think?"

"I'm up for a little artistic expression." Asha laughed, shaking her spray paint can and waggling her eyebrows.

"I kind of feel like smashing stuff," Jax added. That actually sounded pretty good to me, too.

Jin wanted to explore and find new chest locations, even if they were already opened, to keep in mind for next time. "Sounds like we have a plan," he said. "Makes my job as squad leader really easy. I almost feel guilty."

"You shouldn't feel guilty at all. Playtime can be just as important as focused work time, Jin," I explained. Being squad leader all the time was exhausting. I was glad I could delegate responsibility to the rest of the team when we were doing workouts and minor battles. They felt like they were gaining leadership experience, which in a way they were. For me, though, I got a much-needed break. Even a squad leader needed time to hack at things with a pickaxe and follow someone else's lead for a change.

We trotted past the Pass-N-Gas station, which still cracked me up (who doesn't love a good fart joke?) and went behind it to the football field. "Do you guys play soccer?" Jax asked. Right, that's what Americans called it. I shook my head. Organized sports weren't big where I came from. Not getting any takers, Jax headed over to a house that had gotten partially crushed by a tree. "Anyone mind if I smash this house to bits?" he asked.

"I'll join you," I replied, hacking at the football field bleachers with my pickaxe on the way to meet him.

Asha went off to tag a white-walled house down the block, and Jin headed into a nearby building to begin his search.

We swung our pickaxes at the house until there

was nothing left but rubble. The hour passed too quickly for my liking, and soon a message flashed onto my visor screen that the storm eye was about to shrink and we should head to the center of the island for avatar pickup.

Back in the avatar room at HQ, we climbed out of our control pods, stretching our muscles and getting used to being back in control of our own bodies. I no longer had a headache after being jacked into the avatar controls, but my muscles still got sore and I always came back super hungry.

"What's next?" Asha asked me. I was back to being the leader.

"Lunchtime, thank goodness!" I replied. We exited our squad control room and walked out of the Avatar Control room at the same time as Blaze and her team. They looked angry.

"What kind of stunt were you and your team trying to pull down there, Zane?" Blaze demanded.

"You came after us, remember? We didn't even fight back," I replied.

"That's not what I meant and you know it," Blaze growled. "One of you guys buffed up and griefed her, and now her suit is trounced!"

"Not sure what you said there, Blaze, but that wasn't one of us in that built-up power suit," I replied. "Is your teammate okay?"

"Yeah, she'll be fine, but that's not the point." Blaze rolled her eyes. "Anyway, I should have known you guys weren't the PKer type—that's a player killer, if you're not up on the lingo. I almost respected you for what you did, even though it made me really angry." She and her squad pushed past us. "Well, if you find out who it was, you tell them that I'll find out and that I'll be coming for them."

The hallway was crowded with the rest of the cadets heading to lunch, so we all fell in and followed the flow of traffic. It was interesting that Blaze and her team had no idea who the mystery player was either.

I wouldn't have put it past HQ to plant an invincible obstacle just to see how we would handle it, but it didn't add up in this situation. Avatars were expensive. There's no way they would trash one of them on purpose. Jin thought it was an alien or monster, which seemed like a childish explanation, in my opinion. If you can't understand something, just call it a monster.

Jax's theory was the most interesting, and I think the most likely. My guess was that it was a mutant, too. Back when the meteor hit the island a long time ago, many people died, and others who hadn't been exposed when it hit were taken off the island, cured, and relocated. But even though the meteor had hit the prison, no one ever mentioned what happened to the inmates. The government had already lost so much money to tourism and then recovery efforts. My guess was they didn't want the added expense of taking care of the inmates, too. My parents thought they were left there to be destroyed in the acid rain that swept through the island. There was a cha... that not all of them died. I mean, little things were changing on the island all the time. Who was doing it? Our avatars only caused temporary damage, like when we shredded abandoned houses with our pick-axes or built towers to glide off of. When the rain came, it all got swept away like it never happened. My guess was someone was living down there, and whoever it was had to be pretty strong—and adapt-able—to survive.

The rebels back home did have some evidence that something weird was going on. One of our own—a rebel named Ingrid—had been imprisoned there when the comet hit. She had been sending regular updates through our secret network, but those stopped for good right after the first acid rain-storm, even after communication with the island started up again. The rebel in me wanted to get to the bottom of what happened to them, but the new me—the Zane who signed up for life as a Battle Royale trainee to see what life is like when you follow the rules—just wanted to be a normal teen for once. I didn't want to be solving mysteries or out chasing monsters like one of the Scooby-Doo gang. So I decided not to tell my squad mates what I knew. At least not yet.

CHAPTER THREE: ASHA

Lunchtime was rushed, which put me in a bad mood. I tried to stay cheerful to keep everyone else's spirits up like I always did, but I was grumpy on the inside where it mattered most. I was a few bites into my first taste of jambalaya—a spicy New Orleans stew—when the call went out for the afternoon Battle Royale. Weren't we ever going to get a break?

I managed to wolf down the rest of my stew and burned my tongue in the process, then jogged to catch up with the rest of my squad. "Training is a lot harder than I thought it would be," I said when I caught up to them. "We never have a moment to ourselves."

"Maybe next playground session, we can take a break and do nothing at all," Zane suggested. "I'd like to see the island as a tourist for the day."

"Nice thought, but Velasco won't go for that.

They're always watching us," Jax growled. "Don't you remember what we found in his office? That one-way mirror was also a one-way observation window, and our neighbor Kevin warned us they're even spying on us in our quarters."

"We gave up our freedom when we agreed to join up," Zane reminded us.

"Some of us haven't had a taste of freedom for a long time," Jax said. We all got quiet after that. None of us wanted to bring up Jax's criminal past. Whatever each of us had been through before, we were a team now and none of that mattered while we were down here.

I caught sight of Blaze as we entered the avatar room. She saw me too and then turned away. She hadn't been friendly when we were squad mates, but now that we had voted her out, she was just plain hostile.

I hadn't had any experience with people like Blaze back home in my small village. Life was hard enough without picking fights with each other. We all worked together. Teamwork was the only way we could all survive. Then I came here and met Blaze. She tried to take charge from the start, ordering us around even though she was just as clueless and new as we were on that first day. Blaze thought we pushed her out because we had a problem with her power and military training. The truth was her ego was just so big, there wasn't room for anyone else in our squad when she took charge.

I looked over at her team filing into their control room, following behind her in a row like it was a military exercise. I was glad she found a good fit, but it bugged me that she still had an issue with us.

We jacked into our controls and found ourselves in position back on the Battle Bus. Zane was our leader this round since it was an official battle. We had gone over the strategy at lunch and decided on a "path of least resistance" plan. We'd land in the center of Tilted Towers in a power play and search for a chest, then follow the storm eye up to Loot Lake or down to Shifty Shafts, depending on where the storm was headed. It was nice to have a go-to battle plan when we weren't feeling up for the fight. It felt like when I used to play rugby back home. We had a plan for every occasion, and with a lot of practice, things flowed more easily.

Zane gave the signal to jump, so we all got ready. As I leapt from the plane, I caught Blaze's eye. "You're going down!" she mouthed. I knew she meant she had it in for us, but it was pretty ironic since I was about to literally go down as I jumped from the plane. I gave her a thumbs-up and laughed all the way down.

We hit the ground running. I left the group to scout for chests, certain there would be one in the middle of the trees next to the park. I found the chest where it almost always was and saw it was filled with awesome loot. This was going to be a lucky battle. I could just feel it.

From the commotion of happy sounds in my communicator, I could tell my squad mates were getting just as lucky. Jax already had an elimination by picking someone out of the sky on the way down, and Zane had scored a cache of supplies. Jin chugged a shield, and I threw together a small shelter so we could regroup if we needed to.

A shot whizzed past my head as I was going for a spike pad. I wheeled around and saw it was one of Blaze's teammates. There were other cadets nearby, but this girl was gunning for me on purpose. I tried to get her back, then saw Blaze run at me from the side. She had hoped to attack me in my blind spot. I could see they were teaming up against us specifically. A bold move but a bad tactical mistake. Focusing on any single team to wipe them out was a surefire way to get knocked out quickly.

"I'm getting ganged up on here, guys," I called into my com as I tried to knock Blaze back and run for cover. Sniper fire came from the north, hitting Blaze's teammate and knocking her down. "Thanks for the quick cover, Jax," I shouted.

"Wasn't me. I'm fighting one of Blaze's teammates," Jax replied.

"Me too," Jin echoed. I felt badly he was caught in a fight, but was glad he wasn't off looking for imaginary mutants. We didn't have time for that in battle, and it was good that Jin knew his conspiracy theories would have to wait until our next playground event.

Zane ran up from the south, carrying a SCAR. "Sorry I'm late. I picked this awesome weapon off a poor kid who got teamed up on. What'd I miss?"

"Blaze and her gang of merry cadets were after me. If you guys didn't cover me, who did?" I asked, looking around.

A cosplay girl dressed all in white high-fived me as she ran past. That told me who, but my next question was why. She looked familiar, but I couldn't place her. I had a great memory for maps but a terrible one for faces.

"You're teamed up with Zoe again?" Zane asked in disbelief. "Last time you guys met up, she double-crossed you,"

Oh, so that's who she was. "Right. I ended up beating her to the chest we were racing toward. I think she's the one who had my back with Blaze's team." I didn't have time to think about it because Blaze was back with a legendary SCAR and was headed right for me. Zane tossed me a shield potion, and I ducked for cover while I drank it, hoping I'd finish in time.

That's when I blacked out.

I woke up a few moments later, thanks to Zane's quick response, and jumped back into the game. This was no run-of-the-mill battle. We were going to have to work for it, not just to keep our place in the rankings at this level, but to defend ourselves in Blaze's grudge match.

The storm eye was closing in on Loot Lake, so that's where we headed, running across the lake and covering each other as we reached the tower—our favorite perch to pick off lake runners and defend ourselves from snipers on the shore.

Overall, we had a respectable battle. We came in third out of twenty-five teams, and we each raked in a fair number of eliminations before it was all over. Blaze's team came in fifth, thanks in a large part to Zoe's efforts to take out Blaze.

When we climbed out of our pods at the end of the battle, we all started talking at once.

"What was up with Blaze targeting our squad?" Jin was outraged.

"And what was with Zoe coming to our rescue?" Zane asked. He had gotten off on the wrong foot with that girl the first day, and none of us trusted her for a second. "I hope she doesn't think that we're friends now."

"I hope she doesn't think we owe her for that rescue," I replied.

"You guys ever heard the saying 'the enemy of my enemy is my friend'?" Jax chimed in. "Zoe has a powerful team. They came in ahead of us but didn't attack us. That's gotta count for something."

I hated to admit it, but he was right. We needed to play nice with Zoe and her team. At least for the time being.

CHAPTER FOUR:
JAX

I was pumped up after this last battle. I don't know why, but winning just brought out this energy in me. I had to do something to let it out or I was bound to get into a fight.

When I was a kid, my temper was pretty out of control. Someone would interrupt me while I was playing a video game or would cut in front of me in line, and I'd go all animal on them, yelling and even starting fistfights. When I was about twelve, my dad took me aside and told me that wouldn't fly anymore. I was getting too big, and my punches were getting too powerful. If I didn't stop, I'd hurt someone.

Fortunately, instead of telling me to stop fighting, he brought me to a gym, put me in front of a punching bag, and said, "You feel like hitting something, hit this and only this. Anything else is gonna land you in a heap of trouble."

I ended up in a heap of trouble anyway, but at least it wasn't for fighting. Training down here offered a lot of physical outlets for all my extra energy. When my team headed back to the barracks to chill out for a brief break before dinner, I went down to the gym.

I started out by jogging a few laps around the training room. The white noise of the machines in the next room was loud enough to drown out other voices and helped clear my head. Once I got my heart rate up, I did some hurtle sprints. Jin was teaching me parkour during our scheduled training time, and I was starting to get the hang of the jumps. It felt good to fight gravity and win for a change. I was looking forward to learning his Spider-Man wall crawl. That was bound to come in handy back at home after my year of training was over.

When I rounded the corner, I got the wind knocked out of me and fell to the ground. Surprised, I looked around to see what obstacle I had bumped into, but it was no obstacle. Blaze was standing there, hands on her hips, staring down at me with a nasty smile on her face. "Oh, I'm sorry, was I in your way?"

I stood up and glared at her, then walked off as

calmly as I could. It took all my resolve not to hit her back.

I hadn't gone far when one of her squad mates jumped down from a nearby tower and landed in my path. I turned to walk around her. "Excuse me," I mumbled.

"There's no excuse for you, or for what you did to Blaze," she replied. "Your squad is a pack of losers without her. And now we're here to make sure you don't beat us again." With that, she stuck out her leg and tripped me. I hit my head on the side wall, then fell to the ground. I raised myself up on my elbows but decided not to get up just yet. It was clear they weren't going to let me go without a fight and I needed a moment to cool down.

Next thing I knew, Blaze was standing over me. "You and your squad of Impossibles are going down, Jax. We can't have you standing in our way." She moved aside to give me room to stand up. Maybe I could get away from this without a confrontation, I thought, but realized right away I was wrong. She reached up and grabbed me by my shirt collar. "You and your little team need to stand down. You don't need this win like I do. You owe me that at least."

I wrenched away from her and took a step back. "I don't owe you anything. You failed on your own, just like you lost on your own in every battle. Don't put this on me or my squad," I growled.

"I can see you need more convincing, Jax." She motioned to the other girl who had been standing by like a bodyguard. The two of them came at me at once. I crouched low and steadied my legs for impact, grateful my years of training had built in me a solid fighting instinct. I blocked Blaze with my left arm, then struck the girl coming at me while she was off balance. My pent-up energy found an outlet as I struck out at both of them until they finally stopped coming at me. Neither of them had landed a single punch. I wiped the sweat from my palms, then closed my eyes and took a deep breath, finding my center as Asha had taught me the day before when she was explaining meditation to us. When I opened my eyes, I was face-to-face with Officer Gremble. As in THE Officer Gremble who was in charge of my "sentence" here and had the power to send me to juvenile detention. As in THE Officer Gremble who was friends with Blaze's father.

My shoulders sagged, and I let out that deep breath I had been holding. "This was a setup, wasn't it?" I asked quietly.

"Come with me," he said simply and led me out of the training room.

We walked in silence through the maze of hallways to the locked door that led to the main offices of HQ. My squad and I had been sent here once before when we were in danger of getting sent home, and we were warned that it was our last chance.

It had been my last chance and I blew it.

Gremble placed his hand on the sensor, and the door opened with a click. We left the stark, military-style area, and the sounds of our footsteps were instantly muffled in the plush carpet of the HQ offices. The halls were empty, but the offices on each side were filled with people going about their business. Most of the doors were open, and I caught snippets of conversation as I passed. Not enough to make out anything specific. But when Gremble stopped to chat with a junior officer, I heard something that stopped me in my tracks.

"What if we could help him return to his home planet?" one voice asked. *They couldn't be talking about the mysterious cadet . . . could they?* I kept listening.

"It's clearly hostile, and there's no way to communicate with it. We'll have to take it out," the next voice replied.

"We could get the cadets to do it . . ."

"You there! Jaxon!" Gremble shouted, and I looked up. "Let's go." I reluctantly trotted off after him, even though I had already gotten more than enough information.

It was a real alien. Jin was actually right. My head

was spinning. I tried to call up what we saw and experienced down on the island and to combine it with what I had just heard. I didn't have much time. We stopped at a door labeled "CONFINEMENT." Gremble opened the door and motioned for me to get in. I took a deep breath. So this is what it was leading to. I guessed it wouldn't matter what I had overheard. I'd never get a chance to tell my squad mates. I'd get sent to detention, and they would never know.

"Am I—" I started to ask what I was in for, but Gremble cut me off.

"No questions. Someone will be in shortly." Gremble ushered me into the room, then closed the door behind me, locking it from the outside with a key.

I surveyed the room. It actually seemed kind of nice. It looked like a picture I had once seen in an ad for a fancy hotel room. Minus the TV and window, of course. The good part was I had a comfortable bed in an air-conditioned room with a private bathroom, and there was even a sitting area and table in a separate living space. On one hand, this seemed like a place someone could be held in custody for quite a while. On the other hand, if I were to be kept here for a while, that would mean I wasn't getting sent to a detention facility. There were more pluses and minuses to count, but I was running out of hands to count them on.

There was a knock on the door, then a rattle of keys. The door opened, quickly ending the guessing portion of this strange game.

Velasco entered wearing his official military uniform. I wasn't sure whether to be honored to have attracted the attention of the head of the entire facility or scared, but his expression seemed kind compared to the last time he had called me into his presence, and I somehow felt reassured.

"Jaxon," he addressed me in an official tone, then added, "may I call you Jax?" I nodded. He sat down in one of the plush chairs and motioned for me to do the same. "Do you know why you're here?" he asked kindly.

From my extensive experience getting in trouble with the authorities at school and with the police, this was usually a trick question. I also knew that if I didn't answer, he would answer for me. Which he did. "You're here because you seem to be having a difficult time fitting in with some of the other cadets."

Tell me something I don't know, I thought to myself. Outwardly, I just shrugged. I had been tagged as a troublemaker before I arrived, and this wasn't my first offense. There wasn't anything I could say that would change his mind about me at this point.

"You're not going to defend yourself?" Velasco prodded me. I shook my head. He pulled out a view

screen from inside his jacket and pressed a few keys.
A still image of the training gym came up onscreen.
"Do you recognize this place?" I nodded. "You're a
guy of few words, Jax." He laughed. "It's the training
gym, isn't it? The one you were just in when Officer
Gremble came to get you." I nodded. "Did you
know we have cameras there?" I nodded again. He
touched the screen, and a video began to play. They
had taped my entire interaction with Blaze and her
squad mate. Not only that, but the camera followed
us around the room. Either the cameras had motion
sensors, or someone was actually hired to track our
movements to capture whatever they found interesting. The scene played out as they continued to
taunt and bait me until I finally lost control. When
Gremble approached me, Velasco pressed the screen
to stop the replay.

"What happened in there, Jax?" Velasco asked
softly.

"They baited me, sir. I didn't go in there looking
for a fight," I said.

"You're right. None of this was your fault, yet you
didn't defend yourself until you were in danger just
the way you're not defending yourself now," Velasco
replied. "You're a tough-looking kid from a tough
neighborhood with a bad reputation. People are
going to assume the worst of you unless—or until—
you prove them wrong. If you stay silent, you won't

have a shot at changing anyone's mind." He stared at me and waited for a response, but I couldn't think of anything to say. Was he saying it was my fault I kept getting into trouble because people just assumed I was bad? I came from a place where defending your actions was seen as a weakness. I looked down on people who stammered their way through apologies and explanations. I was not going to be one of those whiny babies who begged others for forgiveness.

Velasco could see he wasn't going to get anything out of me with this line of conversation. He sat back and rubbed his neck. The same gesture I always used when I wasn't sure what to say or felt uncomfortable. Could it be that I was making him feel uncomfortable by keeping quiet?

He took a deep breath and leaned forward, trying again. "You gotta work with me here, kid," he pleaded. "I like you, Jax. Reputation aside, you've been nothing but a good kid here. You follow rules. You don't start fights. You don't come with a whole lot of baggage or drama like some of the other cadets. You have the makings of a great soldier. But if you're going to make it here, you need to do one thing." He paused to see if I was listening. "Do you want to know what that one thing is?"

I nodded. "Still not saying anything, huh?" He laughed. "This is gonna be harder than I thought. What you have to do is open your mouth. Stand up for yourself. I know in some places, that's seen as a weakness. But this is the military. The only way you're going to get respect is if you earn it. Don't be anyone's punching bag." He looked me in the eye. "Can you do that, Jax?"

I nodded, then smiled, realizing I was contradicting myself. "Does that mean I'm not in trouble for what happened back at the training gym?" I asked.

"Of course not. We encourage a little healthy rivalry on and off the battlefield. We don't have any real enemies yet. That's why we have you practicing safely against each other. And why we monitor your interactions so closely on and off the battlefield." Velasco smiled and stood up. I remained seated, not sure what would happen next. "You like this room, Jax?"

I nodded, then replied, "Yes, sir. It's the nicest room I've ever been in, actually."

"How would you like to stay here tonight?" he asked, then clarified when he saw my reaction. "Oh, you're not in trouble. I just meant as my guest. You can order whatever you want for dinner, and I can send in a television monitor. Treat it like a mini vacation for the evening."

"You mean I'd be locked in the room alone all night?" I asked.

Velasco walked over to a door that I had thought was a closet and opened it into a common room where three cadets were playing cards. They looked up and waved, then went back to their game. "We're trying out a new program where we bring in cadets for a little break if the training gets to be too much. You've already met Kevin." Sure enough, I recognized the kid from the squad next door. "And that's Liam and Aron." He closed the door, leaving us alone in the hotel room again. "You're free to hang out anywhere in this area tonight, and you're under no obligation to spend time together or make conversation. Would you like to stay?" I nodded, and Velasco laughed. "I'll take that as a yes, as long as you promise to work on speaking in full sentences next time we meet. Is that a deal?" We shook hands on it and he left the room, closing the door behind him.

As soon as I was sure he was gone, I stood up and locked the door to the common room and stretched out on the bed with a happy sigh. I wasn't going to let anything or anyone spoil my first ever vacation.

CHAPTER FIVE:
JIN

It was strange heading into battle without Jax. While we didn't trust him at first, in the past couple of months he had become an important team member. We had come to rely on him as much as we relied on each other.

The last time we saw him, he was headed to the gym after the last battle, just like he often did to blow off some steam. But instead of hearing him come in just before lights out, Officer Gremble had stopped by to let us know Jax would wouldn't be coming home, and he couldn't tell us when he would be returning. The three of us spent most of the evening coming up with theories why Jax wasn't there, but in the end we all agreed he had probably finally gotten in trouble.

We jacked into our pods and found ourselves

on the Battle Bus. I glanced around to see what our competition looked like for this battle. Blaze's team was in the corner, huddled up to plan their strategy, no doubt. Kevin and Malik from next door were goofing around with their two squad mates. Zoe and her squad were directly across the aisle from me. She looked up and caught my eye, then gave me a nod. Were we friends now? I knew she had a beef with Blaze. *The enemy of my enemy is my friend*—the old saying popped into my head. I guess I had been paying attention in history class after all. I was glad to have an alliance with anyone, although Zoe had already proven herself to be an unreliable ally. She had double-crossed Asha in one of our first battles. We would have to watch our backs.

While everyone else around us on the bus was joking around or strategizing with their teams, the three of us sat silently, missing our fourth member, hoping that Jax would be coming back to us soon, or indeed, at all.

Zane caught my attention and signaled our drop point at Salty Springs. I wondered if Zane had picked it because it was Jax's favorite spot. Jax said he liked it because the popular drop spot always guaranteed him some early game action, but I think it was more than that for Jax. More than once, I'd caught him standing behind a tree, staring across the green at the big red house. I didn't see anything special about the house. It looked like an ordinary spot for an ordinary family to live in. I didn't know much about Jax, but I would have bet my spot in the rankings that he did not come from a normal family or live in a house like that.

I landed next to the small gray shed and smashed my way in, hoping to pick up a quick weapon and some healing supplies. I knew Asha was going for the big gray house nearby. She liked to land on the roof and crash her way down, while Zane liked to land on the ground and loot his way up the first house he saw.

I found a spike trap right off the bat and took it as a lucky sign that this would be a good battle for me. I didn't really believe in superstitions like that. At least not like my grandmother did—she would never give people she loved shoes as a gift because she said it would make them run away. She wouldn't speak to my brother for a week after he bought me a pair of shoes for my birthday. To be fair, I left for Battle Royale at HQ a month later, so maybe there was something to it after all. I kissed my pinkie for extra luck, then broke through a nearby door and collected more supplies.

A crash to my left alerted me to someone's clumsy presence nearby. I took them out quickly, then gathered their loot.

"Nice shot!" Zane called out over my com. I

realized it was the first time any of us had spoken since we had jacked in. It was funny how Jax was the least talkative of all of us, but with him gone, we had all become silent.

I went back to collecting supplies and getting the lay of the land. I ducked a few shots without firing back and made my way to the red house Jax was so interested in. I drew my weapon and went inside as quietly as I could, checking out the rooms to my right and left before heading upstairs. I dropped the spike trap behind me to make sure I wouldn't be followed, then focused my attention on the upper floor. I opened the door to the right and jumped back.

"Watch where you're pointing that thing!" Jax yelled, grabbing hold of my weapon. "You could hurt someone with that."

"Jax!" Asha called over the com. "Is that you?"

"Yeah, he's here," I replied, catching my breath. "I thought I was toast when I opened the door and he was standing there." I stuck out my hand and Jax shook it. "Welcome back, man!"

"Thanks. Reunion's over, though. Let's take this place." Jax looked both ways, then darted out into the hall. I was happy to follow him.

I heard a commotion downstairs, then saw a message flash onscreen confirming that I had taken out two players with my spike trap. "Nice going," Jax said.

We collected as much as we could and covered each other as new enemies dropped in around us. As good as it felt to run through Salty Springs solo, it was good working together, too.

We got to the roof and I threw up a ramp. Jax and I built a tower and sniped a few unlucky guests in our backyard. I saw Asha and Zane were nearby and suggested to Jax that we go join them and explore together. "Good idea. I know just where we should all go . . . Haunted Hills."

"Why do you want to go back there?" I asked, remembering our recent unfortunate adventure there.

"I think we should give it another look, in case we find your blobby pink alien friend," said Jax. I couldn't read his avatar's expression, obviously, but it didn't feel like he was mocking me.

"Why would you want to do that?" I asked cautiously.

"I overheard something at HQ that makes me think you may have been right about what you saw."

"We probably shouldn't be talking about this online, folks," Zane's voice cut in. "The walls have ears, as we've found out. But let's head over there and see if we can find our friend, the visitor. Defensive positions only. Sound good?"

"Sounds good to me," Asha chimed in. "I'll tag

a few spots on my way over . . . just for fun and practice."

We spent the rest of the time searching for signs of the mysterious fighter who had caused such a stir last time we were in the area, but we didn't find anything. Not even a clue. When the storm eye started to shrink, we jumped back into the fight. We ran toward the eye, taking cover in bushes and inside forts, but the fire had gone out of us for racking up eliminations. We were all thinking about the visitor and wondering what Jax had heard, and it made offensive strategies difficult.

We ended up coming in fifth place out of twenty, which seemed respectable until you saw our elimination count. It was low. Embarrassingly low. There was no chance that would go unnoticed by the big bosses or by our competition.

Sure enough, as we were exiting the avatar room, Blaze's teammate threw in a dig. "Did you enjoy your little 'camping' trip?" she gloated, referring to our defensive positions for most of the battle.

None of us dignified her with an answer, but as Jax and Blaze passed each other, we could see the tension between them. "What was that about?" I whispered to Jax once we had passed them and were caught up in the rush of kids headed for the mess hall.

"I'll tell you once we get to someplace out of earshot," Jax replied.

We hadn't gone far when I heard someone call Zane's name. I turned to see that it was Zoe. She was standing with her hands on her hips, looking annoyed, as usual. "The alliance is off."

"I didn't know there was an alliance," Zane replied.

"Don't try to out-cool me. I invented cool!" Zoe stamped her foot. "We only make pacts with winners, and you are clearly a team of losers. You didn't even try through most of that battle. We were under attack, and you weren't anywhere to be found. Were you taking a little mini vacation while the rest of us battled?"

Zane shrugged. "Well, if that's the way you feel, I guess it's every squad for itself, right, team?" He looked at us for confirmation, and we all nodded.

"We will see you on the battlefield," Zoe shot back. She was gone with a flick of her ponytail, and her squad followed along behind her.

Instead of turning toward the cafeteria, Jax headed to the battle gym and the rest of us followed. We were all eager to learn where he had been all night and what he'd overheard at HQ.

Without a word, we entered the battle gym. Asha and I circled the perimeter in opposite directions, meeting back at the entrance and giving the all-clear sign. Then we climbed up to our usual perch where Jax filled us in on all he had seen and heard in his time out. We couldn't stay too long. Controlling our avatars in a Battle Royale not only takes its toll on the body, it also makes me really hungry. Plus, I needed time to process all that Jax had told us.

We grabbed our meals to go and headed back to our rooms to get ready for the afternoon's exercises. When we got to our door, we discovered it had been vandalized. "Someone scratched marks in our door!" Asha yelled.

"My guess is Blaze," Jax said flatly. "She knows where we live. and she totally has it out for us."

Zane looked closely at the marks on the door. "Looks like it was done with a sharp object. Carved it right in there."

I took a step back and looked at it from a different angle. Something about it seemed strange. "It looks kind of… neat and purposeful, doesn't it?" The marks were a series of dots and dashes . . .

.‾ ....‾ ‾... ...‾‾ ‾... ....‾ ‾... .....

"It's Morse code!" Zane realized it the same moment I did.

"Can anyone read it?" I asked hopefully.

"I'm the son of rebel spies. I learned code-breaking before I could do math," said Zane.

CHAPTER SIX: ZANE

The code translated easily to coordinates, which clearly meant spots on the Island Map. A4 was in no-man's land: the edge of the island above Snobby Shores and west of Haunted Hills. B3 translated to Haunted Hills proper. B4 and B5 were unexplored territory. We had never been to that area, but that was definitely going to change as quickly as we could get down to the island. We had been looking in the right area before. Maybe someone had spotted us there, and this was a message we had been caught. Or maybe someone wanted us to go there. But who? We had to get back down to the island as quickly as possible and see what was waiting for us at those coordinates.

"We have to clear the message off the door as quickly as possible," Asha said. "If Zane could pick it out this fast, others could break the code with a little work as well. Lucky for us, most folks are still at lunch."

Jax opened the door and went inside. Leaving in the middle of a major crisis was pretty antisocial behavior, even for him, I thought to myself. But he surprised me by coming back with an armload of art supplies. "You like tagging stuff," he said, offering a spray paint can to Asha. "Now's your chance."

Asha took the paint but hesitated. "We could get into a boatload of trouble . . ." she began.

"Our door is already trashed. We'll have to take the fall for it if we want to keep it a secret from Gremble and Velasco," Jax said flatly.

Asha looked to me for confirmation, and I nodded. "Jax has a good point. Have at it!"

She broke into a wide grin, then closed her eyes for a moment before opening the can and letting the paint fly. Her movements were quick and confident. We all took a step back to give her room and watched as the design began to reveal itself on the door. When she was done, she closed the last paint cap with a satisfying click and turned to us. Her face was suddenly filled with uncertainty. She was worried we wouldn't like it.

"It's brilliant!" I said, giving her a big hug. And it truly was a work of art. There, in front of us, our door shouted to the world that we were the Impossibles in big, bold, graffiti-style letters in red, black, white, and green—the colors of Asha's native country.

We didn't have much time to celebrate or congratulate her before reality set in. Kevin and Malik were returning from lunch, munching on brownies and recapping scenes from their recent battle when they stopped in their tracks. "You are going to be in such big trouble." Malik said, his eyes wide.

"That is a bold move, even for a rebel," Kevin added, looking at me. "You really are a risk-taker, I have to hand it to you."

"You're not going to tell, are you?" Jin asked. He was obviously already regretting our group decision.

"You can't keep anything that bold a secret, man," Malik said, shaking his head. He and Kevin walked into their quarters calling out, "Good luck," just before the door closed behind them.

"It certainly was a bold move," I began.

"Yes, it certainly was," an official-sounding voice chimed in from behind me. I wheeled around to see Velasco standing there, looking at the door with his brows knitted together. "You certainly have an eye for design, Asha. Although I would have preferred you decorate the *inside* of your quarters and leave the outside alone. But apparently our instructions weren't specific enough on that point." He jotted something down on his tablet. I would have thought he'd be the type to use an old-fashioned pen and paper to take notes. "That was our mistake. I'll have to change that in the rulebook this afternoon."

"So we're not in trouble, then?" Jin asked cautiously.

Velasco shrugged. "Nothing in the rules says you can't do it, though I wouldn't have made such a daring choice. We keep everything uniform for a reason here in the military. Safety is one reason. Artistic taste is another."

That sounded like a major diss in any language, but Asha took it in stride. She straightened herself up to her full, pint-sized height and responded with a challenging stare. "Did you come here to disparage my artwork, or did you stop by for another reason?" Major props to Asha for being one bold, tiny sheila.

The officer actually looked amused, if not impressed by her challenge. "Actually, I came to let you know your squad is locked out of playground this afternoon."

We let out a collective groan of dismay and outrage. "Why?" I demanded.

"The stats show you had some early eliminations, then you camped in the outskirts avoiding the action for most of the rest of the battle. Your hit-to-shot ratio was poor, and your eliminations were low, showing your skills were sorely lacking." He tapped his tablet for emphasis. "Everything you do down there is recorded and monitored, Zane. You, of all people, should know we're always watching. Each battle costs the military money. If you're going to waste it, we're going to limit your time down there."

Velasco looked at each of us as if he was calculating something or waiting for a reaction. I wasn't going to stick my neck out to challenge him again. We were in enough hot water as it was. He continued. "If there's nothing else, you'll excuse me. I have to deliver the bad news to the three other teams that performed even less admirably than you did."

Sergeant Velasco turned to leave but stopped when Jax stepped forward. It stopped me in my tracks, too. "Actually, sir, there is something else." Velasco paused, waiting for Jax to continue. "I'd like to make a case for extra playground time for our squad."

"Do tell." The officer raised his eyebrows, his surprise echoing my own. Jax, who never spoke up, was actually challenging the head of the entire program.

"The kids who did the best down there this morning will only do better with more practice, while teams like ours will only do worse if you keep us off the island." Jax had a good point. I nodded to show my support, curious to see how Velasco would respond.

He seemed to consider it for a moment, then jotted another note in his tablet. "Okay, son. I've just assigned you and your squad extra gym time with training challenges. Two hours in the gym should help you get back on track. Check your tablets for your new assignments."

"Unfair!" I shouted, before I could stop myself.

"If you want to get better, you'll have to work harder. Jax is right, Zane." Velasco paused, then pointed to the door, smiling broadly. "You are the Impossibles, after all."

I didn't wait for Velasco to leave. I unlocked the door and slammed it open, then stormed inside, the others filing in more quietly behind me. Then I wheeled on Jax. "What the heck, man? You never open your mouth to defend yourself or us. Suddenly you get a day's holiday and you come back ready to take on the establishment. You got us all detention, and this time they're not going to send us to your swanky resort." I picked up my tablet and checked our new assignments. "We'll be lucky to get half of these challenges completed before our two hours in the gym are up."

Asha placed a firm hand on my arm, keeping me from storming out. "The extra workout time will do us all some good—" she began, but suddenly all of our tablets began to flash yellow. "What's this?"

I hadn't seen it before, but Jin knew what it was. "We just got bumped up to yellow alert, you guys," Jin said. "Looks like there's a threat out there somewhere. But I bet we're the only cadets who have a clue as to what it is."

CHAPTER SEVEN: ASHA

The nerve of Sergeant Velasco, turning his nose up at my artwork! I bet he thought his disapproval would stop me from tagging in the future, but instead it made me want to tag the whole stupid hallway.

I kept it together, though. We needed to focus if we were going to ace the challenges he'd set for us. And speaking of focus, I was having trouble crafting a game plan with Jin completely freaking out over the yellow alert that flashed onscreen for five seconds before switching back to green. It was probably a false alarm. We had them all the time back home. In a high-tech place like this, there were bound to be glitches. My suit, for example, was constantly glitching out and getting me popped out of the game, but I wasn't worried about it. If it had happened to Jin, he'd be banging on the doors at HQ, worried that someone had hacked his avatar.

I needed some space to think. "I'm headed to the gym," I announced, heading to the door. "Our scheduled time is in thirty minutes. Meet you guys there?" They nodded, and I was off.

By the time they arrived at the gym door, I had crafted a plan to knock out multiple challenges in each run, leaving us extra time to strategize about the squishy pink mystery alien Jax and Jin were obsessed with before time ran out. That is, if we passed each run on the first try.

I laced up my boots and was putting my training gloves on when Zane appeared at my elbow. He was looking over my shoulder at the plan I had pulled up on my tablet. "Nice work condensing the challenges so we can cover more ground with each run. Are you sure it's allowed?"

"I got into the program by completing challenges like this, Zane. They put in loopholes so you can find them and use them to your advantage."

"You mean like shortcuts?" Zane asked. "Like when you're playing a video game, and you know there's a glitch that cuts out half the course?"

I laughed and shrugged. I didn't grow up playing video games like most teens Zane knew. It was funny how he seemed so worldly, practically raising himself, but he still had such a narrow view of how things were in the rest of the world. "If that helps you understand it better, sure," I replied. "The way I see it, they build in some shortcuts for us to find, like this one I'm taking advantage of here, and we discover others as happy accidents." I directed my eyes upward toward our private conference area near the machine room, hoping he would understand what I meant. He gave me a quick nod, then let out a fake-sounding sneeze that sounded like he said, "Gotcha." I burst out laughing, but quickly covered it up with a cough. I didn't want to have to try to explain it to our squad mates while we were still under the watchful eye of the overseers.

Of course, we made it through the courses in record time. By the time we were through, I could see Velasco and Gremble, along with two other officers I had never seen before, standing on an observation deck midway up. We had gotten their attention. I just hoped we had also gotten back into their good graces.

After the last run, we climbed up to our usual perch overlooking the gym. "Nice work, you guys. We really rocked that course!" I said, complimenting the team. "You have some radical parkour moves, Jin!"

Jin grinned in response. "Did you guys catch our audience on the observation deck?" he asked.

"I didn't even know there was a platform up

there," Jax admitted. "At least they were watching us IRL—in real life—this time, and not over some hidden camera or behind a mirror."

"We should probably talk about those coordinates, mates. Someone wants us down there either to hurt us or to help us. It's in our best interest to get down there as quickly as possible either way. We just have to be prepared," Zane suggested.

Jax looked like he was about to say something, then stopped. I urged him on. "What were you going to say, Jax?"

He rubbed the back of his neck, then closed his eyes, took a deep breath, and let it out before he spoke. "Something else happened while I was off on my overnight break. Something I didn't tell you about."

Jin leaned in, ready to hear more alien conspiracies, no doubt. "Something about the visitor? Something about a cover-up? Aliens, maybe?"

Jax shook his head. "No, I told you everything I overheard. It was just a conversation I had with Velasco. He . . . he told me I needed to speak up more." I held back a laugh. It was funny that this was a revelation to Jax. He was the quietest, most passive guy I had ever met. "He said that when I don't speak my mind, I end up getting into trouble, and it would help me get along with you guys better if I . . . you know, like . . . talked more." We all nodded silently, not knowing how to respond. "So, you know . . . I'm gonna try. I just want you guys to know it's not like I think I'm better than anyone. I just . . . in my experience, talking gets me into more trouble than not . . . you know . . . saying anything."

Jax looked down at his hands. I felt badly for him. It looked like that speech took a lot out of the guy. I leaned in to give him a hug, then pulled back. "Is a hug too much to ask for?" I asked. He shrugged, so I just gave his shoulder a quick squeeze of support. That would have to do for now.

Just then, the tower we were sitting on started to rumble. None of us had anything to grab onto for support, so we all flailed about wildly as the tower fell. As we were going down, we were pelted with foam darts and felt-tipped arrows from all directions. As I hit the soft, cushioned ground next to my squad mates, I heard wild laughter. I looked up and Zoe's and Blaze's teams were gathered around the four of us.

We had been griefed, plain and simple. They had teamed up on us just for fun. Unfortunately for us, the team of officers was still standing on their observation perch, watching and taking notes. So much for our show of strength in the challenges. If Battle Royale was a carnival ride, today it was a roller coaster, and we had just hit the bottom of the drop. Fortunately for us, the only way to go was up.

CHAPTER EIGHT:
JAX

We hit the ground in a tangled mess of arms and legs. By the time I stood up, Velasco was on the deck ushering Blaze, Zoe, and their goon squad out of the gym. They had been docked from the upcoming island overnight, which was fine by me, but I would have liked a few minutes to get in a few punches before Velasco broke it up. They were lucky he arrived when he did.

When the rest of the crew headed to dinner. I stayed back to punch stuff and cool down. I was glad they gave me my space, especially after my long, awkward speech about needing to talk more. They were probably talking about it as they walked to dinner. Or maybe they hadn't even given it a second thought. Who could tell?

On their way out, I did ask Zane to bring me back a Chicago-style thick crust pizza with extra cheese and hot peppers. I needed some comfort food after everything I had been through lately. Too many fights outside of battle weren't good for my reputation. And as Velasco warned me, if I wanted to clean up my act, I'd have to spend more time proving I was a team player and less time pretending I didn't care about anything or anyone.

I got in a hot shower before the guys arrived with my pizza. Asha had stayed back to tag more doors. That girl made me laugh. The more people tried to take her down, the harder she worked to build herself back up and then go a step further than anyone expected. I had never met anyone like her. Or Jin or Zane for that matter. They were good people. It wasn't easy to open myself up to anyone, but considering I had to be lumped in with three other people for a year, these weren't a bad crew to be stuck with.

Asha met us in the avatar control room covered in paint, still giddy from her tagging adventure. Her positivity was contagious, and even I felt a smile coming on. "You know tagging up here isn't like tagging on the island. On the island it disappears with the acid rain. Here in HQ, that stuff stays long enough to get you in trouble," I warned her.

She just shrugged it off. "Whatever happens, it

was still worth it." She smiled as she climbed into her control pod and jacked in. The rest of us followed her lead.

On the Battle Bus, I looked around and noticed a positive shift in the mood. It might have been because we were all going on the overnight to explore instead of to fight it out. Maybe it was that Blaze and Zoe weren't there and I was projecting my relief on every other face I saw. But maybe the others did feel the same way about those two squads as we did. I always assumed we were the only squad that they targeted, but they could have been acting the same miserable way to all the others as well. I'd have to keep an eye out next time.

We jumped straight to the northwestern shore and instantly set up camp by the first coordinates. It would have been a pretty decent beach, under normal circumstances. I mean, without the acid rain and potential alien invasion. We all collected resources and threw up a fairly strong fort with a good base and a tall observation tower. We figured we would keep at least one person up top and one person down below at all times. Our mission this time around was to spend the night on the island to strategize for future battles and uncover all the secrets we could. It wasn't to shoot at each other or worry about eliminations, but it was still important to keep up a good habit of staying aware of potential enemies at all times.

Once the fort was built, we spread out and started searching for clues, keeping in contact through our coms. As I wandered through the trees, I felt something watching me. It was a familiar feeling. I tried to stay calm as I turned slowly, keeping a tight grip on my weapon.

Sure enough, there was someone standing there. A ghost, as far as I could tell. I mean, she was standing right in front of me, but she wasn't showing up as there on my view screen like all the other cadets. She was wearing a prisoner's jumpsuit and she wasn't armed. I raised my hand slowly, trying to make my greeting look peaceful and nonthreatening. She raised her hand as well, then grabbed my arm and pulled me hard as she ran into the forest.

"HELP!" I yelled into my com. "I'm being kidnapped!" It felt weird saying it, but I couldn't break my avatar free from her strong grasp. All I could do was try to stay upright as she dragged me along with her.

"I'm locking on to your coordinates!" Jin yelled. "I'll be right there!"

"Me, too!" Asha echoed.

Zane ran into view and blocked our path. At the sight of him, my attacker stopped short and let go of me. I dropped to the ground, then scrambled to Zane's side. "Ingrid?" Zane said, his voice a quiet question. He reached his hand out, and she did the same, then they started communicating with each other using hand signals.

"You know this person?" I was completely taken aback. Zane didn't answer but leaned forward to give this stranger a hug. Clearly, they had history.

Jin and Asha arrived. Asha lunged forward, mistaking their hug for an attack. I held her back. "Believe it or not, they know each other."

"She shouldn't be here," Asha said, tapping on her visor. "Ouch! I forgot I'm not wearing a visor. Why do I keep doing that?" She shook her head. "She's not appearing on my view screen. Is it broken again?"

I shook my head. "She's not on mine either." My attacker, whose name was probably Ingrid, took Zane's hand and tugged at him gently, urging him to follow her into the forest. With her other hand, she beckoned the rest of us to follow her.

"Trust me," he said, then put his hand to his lips, then to his ear, then to the sky. It was a clear reminder that we weren't on a secure channel and should keep quiet for now.

"Are you sure it's safe?" I asked.

He nodded and beckoned me to follow.

I looked at Asha and Jin to see what they thought. Jin nodded. He was up for anything that smelled of a mystery. Asha shrugged. "I hope he's right. I don't trust anything that doesn't show up here," Asha said, pointing to her view screen without poking herself in the eye this time.

CHAPTER NINE:
JIN

The path led to a clearing. In the center was a small mountain face that went straight up. It looked like we had hit a dead end, but Ingrid continued to lead us straight toward the mountain. I went to use my pickaxe to chop our way inside, when Ingrid held up a hand to stop me. She tapped a code into a hidden sensor pad and a small door opened, just wide enough for us to enter one at a time.

The mountain was just a façade for a hidden lair. I couldn't believe it! We were probably the first cadets to enter. We were forging new ground! I went to speak, but it seemed my communication link had gone out. My guess was that whatever this place was, it was shielded from the coms.

Inside my control pod, my palms grew sweaty. We had followed this stranger—this potential kidnapper—into a place where we could no longer communicate with HQ or each other. I didn't feel safe, but I was more excited than I had ever been in my life. We followed our guide up more steps than I could keep track of. Eventually the stairwells opened up to rooms that served different purposes. We passed a garage, a hospital or medical lab, sleeping quarters, and at the top, a sort of control room. Purple curtains blocked the windows. I approached one of the windows and drew back a curtain, which revealed an insane view of the entire island laid out below us. This was a fantastic hideout and a great way to keep track of everything that happened down on the island. I wondered if we were safe from the storms in this place.

I felt a tug at my arm and turned to see Zane pointing and staring at someone in a mech suit. They turned slowly, and I had a sinking feeling I already knew what I was going to see. Standing there right in front of me was the mech suit I had seen before with the pink-faced blob of an alien. "No way! It is an alien! I was right," I tried to shout, but my com was down.

Zane tapped his earpiece. He knew I was speaking, but he couldn't hear me either.

Ingrid walked over to a small glowing box on a table and opened it. Inside were four gold, seashell-shaped items, no bigger than marbles. She offered each of us one and then tapped her ear. Zane attached it to the ear of his avatar and smiled, then signaled that we do the same. My hands were shaking as I hooked the earpiece onto my ear.

"Thank you for coming." Ingrid's voice suddenly came in loud and clear. "I hope I didn't frighten you. I can't believe you're here, Zane! Did the resistance send you?"

When Zane realized we were all jacked into Ingrid's system, he turned to address us first. "I don't know how this is possible, mates, but I know this sheila! She was a prisoner on this island. A fellow rebel, she got caught mixing explosive cocktails to blow up a bunch of statues down by the capital. A radical gal, she was also a nice person to hang out with. I thought she was destroyed when the meteor hit the prison," Zane said, shaking his head in disbelief. "Ingrid, meet Jax, Jin, and Asha, my squad mates."

"Nice to meet you all. I'm glad you got my message." She turned to Jax. "I'm sorry about the attack. It was the only way to get Zane here without arousing suspicion. How did you know I was here, Zane?"

"This is a big surprise to me, fair dinkum!" Zane exclaimed. "How'd you smuggle in these coms? I recognize them from the lab back Down Under."

Ingrid was about to answer, but I had to address the issue of the rather large alien standing in front of us. "I hate to interrupt, but does anyone else see the alien standing right here staring at us?" I butted in.

Ingrid nodded. "Yes. This alien is the other part of the reason I brought you here. I call him Mixiplixit. That is the closest I can get to pronouncing his name," Ingrid explained apologetically. The alien nodded as if it had recognized its name.

"And what exactly is Mixiplixit doing here on the island?" I asked, trying to pronounce the jumble of letters that formed his name. "Aside from scaring Jax a few days ago and attacking that girl right in front of us, I mean," I said, recalling the first time we had seen him.

"He's trying to get home, actually," Ingrid said simply. "He usually goes on walkabouts out in the rain, but he had wanted to get a closer look at your avatars and accidentally got a little too close for comfort," she said, looking over at her companion.

While I was busy asking questions, Asha had walked over to the alien and touched the mech suit on the shoulder. In response, the alien touched her suit in the same place. She turned her head to one side, and the alien did the same. It seemed so innocent. Like a game kids would play, trying to mimic each other's movements.

"Where did he come from? And why?" Asha asked, continuing their silent game of follow-the-leader.

Ingrid shrugged. "He seems to be on a research

mission, as far as I can tell. We haven't been able to communicate with words yet. He crash-landed with the meteor. I think he rode in on it, actually. Some of the mutant inmates went after him, but I was able to fend them off. I lost a few good allies in the fight," she said sadly. "It's just me and Mixiplixit now, and I haven't gotten much more out of him. We don't have any real way to communicate."

"I'm sorry, did you say mutants?" Asha asked.

Ingrid nodded. "When the meteor hit, many prisoners died, but some of us survived. Our bodies mutated in order to live through the acid storms. We stayed hidden as the first search parties came down, and I've been living underground ever since." She thought for a moment, then looked at all of us quizzically. "Are you all from the same area of the Outback as me and Zane?" We shook our heads. "Then how is it that all of you speak with such perfect Australian accents?"

"When we arrived at HQ, the government stuffed a universal translator in our ears. They're each speaking their own native tongue, but the translator feeds off the intent of their words, and we end up hearing it in our own dialect," Zane replied, then he smacked his forehead. "Wait a minute! Can you ask him to speak? Maybe we will be able to understand him."

Ingrid called to the alien and the pink blobby brain sprang to life, wobbling and jiggling. I heard a tinny voice speaking as if from far away. "Can you understand me?" he asked tentatively. We all cheered. The brain jiggled again.

"Holy Dooly! Yes, you are coming in quite clearly!" Ingrid sounded shocked and relieved. "Finally, we can understand each other! We don't have much time before we have to send these cadets back and our communication will be cut off again. Can you tell me what you are doing here and what you need? How can I help you?"

"First I must take this opportunity to thank you for taking me in and defending me for so long. Your trust means everything to me," the brain blabbered. "I am not sure how much you have guessed by now, after all our time together. I am an explorer and scientist. I was out collecting research samples on an asteroid when a piece broke off and hurtled me through space. I landed here on your planet. I have only survived because of the wonderful rains that fall each day and night here. They restore my health. I don't know how I'll get home again. I am terribly lost, you see."

That was quite a story. We had a lot to process. I couldn't think of anything to respond. Ingrid was about to come at him with more questions when I felt a rumbling in the ground and saw a flash of light in the distance through the windows. "We have to go," I said, looking at Zane. "We've been here too long already. I wish I could stay. I have so many questions for you, but something's happening out there, and if we're caught with our coms off, we may never get the chance to come back here."

Zane nodded. "I'm sorry, Ingrid and . . . Mixerploozer . . . however you pronounce your name. We do have to leave. I'll try to be back later tonight if we can." He unhooked the golden seashell from his ear, and we hurriedly did the same. Ingrid led us to a door in the side of the mountain and opened it, giving us a salute. We each leaped off the cliff and instantly deployed our gliders.

A few meters into our jump, our coms sprang back to life. "Yellow Alert. Squad I-28, evacuate sectors A and B immediately. Can you hear us? Please respond."

"We are here and we understand," Zane said. "We are on our way to the C zone now."

"Thank goodness you are responding, Squad Leader. Is your team safe?" the voice asked anxiously.

"Yes, ma'am. I'm sorry to have worried you. Our coms were . . . offline," Zane replied calmly. We landed safely on the ground at the edge of Snobby Shores. Zane raised his hand to get our attention then mouthed the words, "Don't reveal anything." We nodded our understanding and let Zane do all the talking.

"Report to the green at Tilted Towers for

immediate avatar retrieval," she directed us. "Your avatars need to be checked for malfunctions."

Zane motioned for all of us to huddle together, then he raised his hand again to get our attention. He moved his avatar's lips silently, saying, "They must have been listening to know our coms went out. Nod if you can understand me." Asha, Jax, and I all nodded. "We need a cover story."

"We could say there was an accident," Asha suggested.

Another accident where we all got mangled at the same time? That didn't sound okay to me. We'd look like fools, just like we did our first time on the island when we all got eliminated with one shot. I shook my head, then raised my hand to speak next, moving my lips without making a sound. "We should say we followed Jax because he sent out a call for help. That was the last thing they heard us say. They will know anything else was a cover-up." They nodded in response.

Jax raised his hand, and we all turned toward him. "I could say I was pulling a prank. They would believe me."

Zane shook his head. "We can't have you taking the fall."

"We could tell them the truth—that our coms went out when we entered the mountain," Asha suggested.

"Too risky. They'd search the mountain," Zane replied. "Let's tell them it was a military exercise and we did it on purpose."

We all nodded and smiled. It was perfect. It contained just enough truth to make it believable without revealing any secrets we felt needed to be kept until we could find out more information. And it made us look pretty fierce, too.

With that, we headed to the rendezvous point and awaited the drones.

CHAPTER TEN: ZANE

When we climbed out of the pods, we were greeted by Velasco and two bulky, uniformed officers who looked like bodyguards. The sergeant was fuming, and the guards seemed ready for a fight. I knew we would be in big trouble if we couldn't talk our way out of this. Luckily, I was pretty skilled at wiggling my way out of sticky situations.

He started in as soon as we were assembled in front of him. "What in the world were you kids doing down there with your coms off?"

"I'm sorry, sir. We should have told you. We were running a military exercise," I said, putting on my most honest and apologetic face.

He narrowed his eyes. "What kind of military exercise?"

"Since we were assured we'd be safe on the island for a few hours, I took the opportunity to stretch our squad's muscles a bit." I paused to see if he was buying it. He didn't interrupt, so I kept going. "Jax agreed to pretend he was being kidnapped, then everyone ran to his rescue. You probably heard that on our coms." Velasco nodded, confirming that they were, indeed, listening to our stream at all times. "When Asha and Jin passed that test with flying colors, I took the next step. I instructed my team to disable their coms to see if we could figure out a way to work together without them,"

"Why in blazes would you do a stupid thing like that? These avatars are million-dollar machines, and we have backup plans for every possible malfunction," he replied.

"I'm sorry to disagree with you, Sergeant, but Asha's com goes out fairly often, and she ghosts onscreen. She basically becomes invisible. Back in the early days, we all got roasted in the acid rain because we didn't have a backup plan. Your team beamed Asha's avatar up, but we weren't alerted and it led to quite the catastrophe," I said. I watched his eyes for a response. If they narrowed into slits, it would mean he didn't believe me. If he rolled his eyes, it would mean he thought I was being an immature kid. But if he raised his eyebrows and nodded, I'd know I had him.

Velasco took his time, looking at each one of us in turn, then gave the raised eyebrow nod. I breathed an inward sigh of relief. To my right, I saw Jin's shoulders relax visibly. I'd have to talk to that kid about keeping his reactions in check next time we had a moment to talk in private. "Well, then, the next time you decide to go off book, you let me in on it first. We're responsible for your safety up here, and we can't be out of communication for even a second."

I had him feeling confident and reassured. Time to do a little digging. "Sir, I do have one question," I said tentatively, trying to sound meek and insecure.

"What is it, son?" Velasco's tone softened.

"Well, it's just that you told us we were safe on the island since there was no threat of rain, and it was just our avatars down there." I paused for effect.

"Yes?" Velasco's guard went up just a touch. I got the sense he knew what was coming.

"You said there were fail-safes built into the avatars, but when you lost track of us on the coms, the base immediately went to yellow alert. It sounded over our com like people were panicking. Why did that happen if we were never in any danger?"

The officer let out a heavy sigh. "Nothing is completely safe, Zane. No one has gone down there since the meteor hit and survived. The island still holds mysteries we don't know about. Nothing to worry about. But still, we have to be on our toes," Velasco replied. He was playing my game, telling enough of the truth that it sounded believable, but molding the rest of it to fit the situation. Unless Gremble knew about the alien and Velasco didn't. And maybe Velasco knew about the prisoners and Gremble didn't. This was becoming a sticky puzzle, and we were right in the middle of it.

"I understand, sir," I replied. "I appreciate your being honest with us about that. We'll certainly be more careful in the future." My squad mates echoed my assurances. Velasco and the muscle twins left, seeming satisfied the conversation had gone in their favor while I counted it as a win in our corner.

It was late as we headed back to our quarters. We were careful to keep the conversation away from any alien or mutant-related topics while the walls had ears. When we got into our room, Jax disappeared into the bedroom and came back with a small machine. He switched it on and it let out a low hum, creating white noise in the background.

"What is that?" I asked.

"Last night before he left me in the private quarters, Velasco asked if there was anything I needed." He shrugged. "I told him you snored like a freight train, and it was keeping me up at night." Jax smiled with a broad, crooked-toothed grin we had never seen before. "I asked for a sound machine to drown you out!" He laughed just then, and Jax and Asha joined in.

I cracked up, too, then sobered up quickly. "Wait a sec . . . do I snore?"

Jin and Jax looked at each other and groaned. "You seriously didn't know?"

I was definitely embarrassed, but at least there was an upside to it. "I'm so sorry, guys! But hey, at least it earned us our own white noise machine so we can talk here in private. Our secret group gym conversations were probably starting to look a little suspicious."

Jax turned up the sound machine, and we all gathered around it, being careful to speak softly. "We should probably address the alien-mutant issue first," I began.

Jin jumped up. "Yes! I told you guys! I knew I was right!"

"Shhh!" Asha pulled him down. "Curb your enthusiasm, Jin! Let's focus on what we know, what we need to know, and what we're going to do about it."

"Okay, so we know that my old buddy Ingrid is alive and generally well, living as a mutant down on the island. She said that there are others like her, but she's working alone with the alien. She also said that there are some mutant prisoners down there who aren't as nice and innocent as my rebel friend," I began. "And it seems like Velasco knows something about the added dangers down there, whether it's just about the alien or the angry mutant prisoners, too."

"We also know that the alien is lost, but we don't know what he, or she, or it needs to get home or how we can help it," Jin added. "The thing is, nothing our avatars do can last on the island. We can only guide and direct Ingrid and Mixiplixit—did I get his name right?" We all shrugged. It sounded right to me.

"The second issue is whether we keep this a secret from the officers," Asha chimed in. "Based on what Jax reported, Gremble knows there's an alien down there, and he knows it needs to get home. But do we let him know that we know?"

"It depends on whether we agree to help him . . . it . . . the alien, I mean," Jax chimed in. "Do we believe what it said? Is it telling the truth?"

"You guys are all talking like rebels now." I laughed. "Thinking the people in charge automatically want to keep secrets from people like us. It sounds like Gremble wants to help the alien get home. Maybe we should tell him we know and offer our assistance," I suggested.

Jin, Jax, and Asha shot down that idea all at once. They were all for keeping it a secret until we knew more. I made my case for telling Gremble and offering our help. There couldn't be any harm in helping someone who was lost get back home. The fact that it was an alien was beside the point. Besides, I had joined up to learn what life was like living inside the law. For once I didn't want to be an outlaw. I wanted to follow the rules and tell the truth, not create more secrets and intrigue.

The only thing holding me back from telling the truth was that I was worried about Ingrid. She needed to stay in hiding, and revealing what we knew could put her at risk, and I said as much to the others. "And what about Jax?" Jin added. "He has a lot to lose if he gets in trouble. Not to mention Asha getting sent home and losing her ticket out of her small hometown." Jin played the sympathy card, and I knew it, but he was still right. "I still vote we keep it our secret. Our really cool, alien, mutant secret!"

"Okay, fine. We'll keep it a secret for now. We just have to decide how to help without getting kicked out of this place or causing more harm than good to Ingrid and our new alien friend." With us all in agreement, we headed off to a much-needed night's rest.

CHAPTER ELEVEN: ASHA

I spent the night dreaming I was being chased by aliens and mutants and Officer Gremble, so I was relieved to hear the sounds of the early wake-up call over the room's speakers. The details of my dream were fuzzy, but there was something itching at the back of my brain—an idea. Something about the communicators.

YES! That was it. I remembered. I banged on the door to the boys' room and let myself in. Jax and Zane were almost ready, but Jin was still in bed. Naturally, I went over and sat on him. "Wake up, lazy bones. I think I've figured it out!"

"Figured what out?" Zane asked.

I reached over and flipped the white noise machine back on, beckoning them to come closer. "My com keeps going out down on the island," I announced. No one reacted. I realized I had to spell it out for them. "When my com goes out, I'm invisible to you and to anyone watching. I can go into that mountain and they won't suspect anything."

"Ohhhh." Zane slapped his forehead. "How did I not think of that before? I guess that makes you our secret weapon, Asha. How quickly can we get back down there? Has anyone seen the schedule yet?"

I picked up the nearest tablet and almost dropped it immediately. "Oh no. This is bad."

"What is it?" Jin jumped out of bed and grabbed his tablet from me. "Oh, this *is* bad. We're headed down to the island for our regularly scheduled Battle Royale, but they are sending down fewer teams, and we will be accompanied by three marshals—extra avatars created to watch over and protect us since we're at yellow alert."

"Does it say who we're up against?" Zane asked, pulling it up on his tablet. "Jeez, Louise! It's us against Blaze and Zoe. They've double-teamed us against the two squads who are probably looking for revenge at this point. They missed last night's sleepover."

"So did we," I pointed out.

"It looks like Gremble and company want to keep us busy," Jax said. "Because if we're busy fighting, we can't go off and explore. My guess is that the marshals are really headed down there to check out the area where we disappeared last night and maybe watch us to make sure we're not doing anything we shouldn't. I wouldn't be surprised if they made the whole A sector of the map off-limits for today's battle."

"I guess they didn't buy our story after all," I said flatly. The others nodded in agreement. "Well, then, let's give these guys a run for their money. Which one of you is going to create the distraction so I can run in and grab those coms?"

"Are you sure you want to do this?" Jax asked.

I nodded without hesitating. "I'm the scavenger and the scout. I'm small and fast, and no one would suspect that I'd go off on my own because I wanted to explore and tag stuff like I usually do. Now what can we use to cause that distraction?"

Jax and Zane looked at each other as if they had the same thought, then both said, "Explosives!" at the same time.

When it all came down to it, it was easier than I had thought it would be to carry out our mission. The marshals onboard gave the Battle Bus an unusually strained mood, and everyone was pretty quiet throughout the ride. We decided to jump quickly and land at Retail Row, one of the farthest places on the map from Haunted Hills, just to throw them off our trail. We headed west almost immediately, though, picking up as many explosives as we could on the way.

As we had predicted, the two opposing squads started coming at us as soon as we hit the island. Jax stood as a long-range guard as the sniper while Zane took care of any close-up attacks. Jin collected supplies and built forts, and I stayed in stealth mode, scouting for weapons and traps. While my squad mates kept the competition off our backs, I stock-piled as many clingers, grenades, and remote explosives as I could, and I even collected a few stink bombs. I handed out the loot, then waved goodbye to my squad mates as I headed for the mountain.

I ran into my first marshal as I passed between Tilted Towers and Loot Lake. "Good morning," he said, giving me a friendly wave.

"Jambo!" I said, noting that my traditional Swahili greeting didn't get translated.

"Careful over by sectors A and B," he said. "Some cadets got lost over there yesterday. Might be a communication dead zone. We have people checking it out."

"Thanks for the warning," I said, feeling relieved. Whoever this marshal was, I wasn't on his radar yet. Any move I got caught making could be passed off as an innocent accident. I turned south after the towers, in case the marshal was watching me, then made my way north after I was sure I wasn't being watched. When I heard the explosions off in the distance, I knew the guys were beginning to launch their distraction plan.

As planned, Zane set off a small explosion by Pleasant Park, trying to attract the attention of anyone on the ground. I could see that one of the enemy squads had been building a pretty tall tower over by Loot Lake. The activity stopped as soon as his explosive went off. Good. We had attracted someone's attention.

As I snuck away toward the mountain lair, I saw three more explosions go off in the direction of Loot Lake. I hoped our diversion was working.

It wasn't long before I saw a familiar orange jumpsuit dart out from under cover and then quickly dart back. I ran toward it, hoping it was actually Ingrid and not some enemy avatar out to get me. I was nowhere near my squad mates and couldn't risk a fatal injury. There was no one around to heal me if I fell.

Fortunately, Ingrid greeted me, and we ran together silently toward the mountain. She opened the door, and we stepped inside. My communicator crackled and died the moment I went in. I motioned to keep the door open so I could keep an eye on the action outside. She nodded and handed me the communicator.

"I'm glad you came," Ingrid said. "When I saw the explosions through the window, I was hoping it was you."

"We don't have much time. We'd like to help, but we don't know how," I said breathlessly.

"Do you know if they know about us up at HQ?" she asked nervously.

I nodded. "I think one of the officers—he's second in command—knows there's an alien here on the ground. He suspects we know something and we're keeping it from him, but he doesn't know what it is yet," I explained. "The good news is that I don't think they know about you or the other prisoners. At least, no one has mentioned it to us."

Ingrid seemed to consider this for a moment. I looked out at the landscape and saw more explosions in the distance and watched idly as a tower fell, hoping it wasn't one of ours. "Did we attract any suspicion yesterday when you were here? How did you manage . . ."

"We told a few white lies. The top guy in charge, Sergeant Velasco, admitted there are things happening here on the island that they don't know about, and he's afraid things could get dangerous. I'm not sure he knows anything more than that," I told her.

"At least I'm safe, but I am worried about my pink friend up there. I wish I could communicate with him. I learned more from those few moments yesterday than in all the months since we've been hiding out here together," she said sadly.

"You are worried for him, but you don't seem to be worried for yourself," I observed.

She shrugged. "I gave up my freedom long before I was caught with those explosives and sent to jail. As soon as I joined the rebel forces . . . well, anyway, now I have a new cause. Right?" she said, her eyes brimming with tears. "I try not to think about it, really." She wiped her eyes and put on a brave smile. "But I'm happy now that I've met you guys. It's nice to have someone to talk to, and it's really nice to have friends I can lean on. It's been pretty hard doing it on my own . . ." She burst into tears and sobbed quietly while I tried to comfort her with an avatar hug. "I'm sorry, I don't usually break down . . ."

A stink bomb went off in the distance. That was Zane's signal it was time for me to leave. "I have to go . . . I'm so sorry." I felt bad leaving her, but if I didn't go, things could be a whole lot worse for all of us.

"When can I see you guys again? To help me translate," she added. She didn't want to admit it would be good for her, too.

"The winners of this battle get playground time alone here tomorrow. If it's us, we'll land on your roof at the top of the mountain," I explained. "Watch for the bus."

I handed her the golden rebel com and stepped out of the doorway. My communicator instantly crackled back to life. I waved to Ingrid, and she waved back before closing the hidden door behind her.

"Hello?" I called out, trying to sound panicked. "Can anyone hear me? I think my suit malfunctioned again." I ran as quickly as I could to get as far from the mountain as possible by the time anyone caught up with me. Fortunately, my avatar moved on the island as swiftly as I could travel in real time. I had reached the easternmost edge of Pleasant Park by the time one of the marshals caught up with me.

"Jambo!" the marshal called out happily. It was the same one I had passed earlier. "I'm here to help." I returned his greeting and jogged over to him. "Where were you when your com went out?" he asked.

"It was way south of here," I lied. "By Greasy Grove. It went out as I was running through the area doing some reconnaissance, and then it went back up somewhere past Tilted Towers. I've been walking around for a while looking for someone to help. I'm glad you found me."

He nodded, then took my arm. "I have one avatar to beam up," the marshal said into his com. "She seems pretty shaken up. She had quite a fright being out here alone with no com," he continued with a wink. "Don't worry, little lady. We'll get you all patched up in no time."

When I climbed out of my control pod, I was greeted once again by Sergeant Velasco. This time Officer Gremble was with him. I was separated from my group, who were still down there engaging in what looked like a really tough battle against Blaze's and Zoe's teams. "Hello there, Asha," Sergeant Velasco said, putting his hand on my shoulder. "Are you okay? Marshal Denis mentioned you looked a little shaken up."

Officer Gremble turned to Velasco and laughed. "I think you and Denis are underestimating our friend Asha here. Aren't they, Asha?"

"I'm sorry?" I asked, trying to keep my voice from shaking. I was worried I had been found out. I would make a terrible spy.

"You're a pretty tough cadet, and this isn't the first time your com has gone out. I'd be surprised if this rattled you at all," he said, looking into my eyes. Did he know? Was he trying to smoke me out or make me crack? He leaned closer to whisper into my ear. "I think you're trying for a little sympathy, aren't you? Maybe trying to land that cushy vacation your buddy Jax got the other day?"

So that's what he thought! I was relieved, and I let it show in my expression. "I really could use a break. We're working pretty hard down here." Sergeant Velasco raised his eyebrows. The last thing I wanted was for him to think I was wimping out of training. Well, actually, the last thing I wanted was for them to find out we were helping an alien and a mutant prisoner stay hidden, but this came in a close second place. "Of course, I can handle it without a break, sir. Everything here really is wonderful. Especially the food! But a night off . . ."

Velasco was about to speak when Officer Gremble cut in. "Request denied," Gremble said sternly. "Head back to your quarters. You can meet up with your squad there once they're done down there. We'll get your avatar checked and make sure it doesn't have any more malfunctions." He touched his ear to activate his communicator. "All marshals head down to the coordinates our cadet just mentioned and search the area for dead zones. We want to make sure we have eyes and ears on every inch of that island at all times."

Gremble switched off his communicator then looked me in the eye. "Did you see anything down there? Anything unusual? Anyone unusual?"

He knew! And by the confused look on Sergeant Velasco's face, Gremble wasn't letting his senior officer in on the secret. "What are you getting at, sir?" I decided to answer his questions with questions for as long as I could. Maybe I'd be able to smoke him out instead.

Just then, Jin and Zane climbed out of their pods laughing. Perfect timing. Their smiles turned grave when they saw me standing with the officers, but I reassured them with a hand gesture while Gremble and Velasco were glancing at the battle scene in the view screen. I looked up just as Jax sniped the last four cadets left on the island and landed us the victory.

"How did you manage that?" I asked, smiling.

"We lured them with those explosives you collected, then sacrificed ourselves, leaving Jax to snipe everyone from a hidden tower." Jin was laughing again.

"You'd think the other teams would have learned that trick by now," Jax said, laughing as he climbed out of the pod. I greeted him with a hug, and he didn't resist for once. Even Officer Gremble and Sergeant Velasco congratulated him on the win.

They escorted him to the center stage of the avatar room, and we all followed along. Jin and Zane looked at me questioningly, and I gave them a subtle thumbs-up. The mission had been accomplished, and it looked like my interrogation was over, at least for the time being.

CHAPTER TWELVE:
ZANE

Our mood on the Battle Bus was festive as we headed down to the playground that morning. We even had a little celebration dance party while we were waiting for our drop. No areas were off-limits, and there were no marshals onboard. Somehow we were in the clear . . . or at least that's what they wanted us to believe. I'm sure they were still watching us closely.

The yellow alert had been lifted once the marshals finished searching the fake coordinates Asha had given them. Asha's suit actually did have a flaw, and they created a temporary patch they hoped would work while we were on the playground, but they advised us to stick together just in case. Something told me that wouldn't be a problem.

We landed at the top of the mountain. Ingrid and

the blobby alien came out to greet us. Asha stepped inside the lair, and her com went out as expected. We stayed outside and waited for Asha's golden seashell communicator to spring to life. As we had planned, she would be our translator inside the lair and send us up notes, just like kids in the movies always passing notes in class.

The plan was to spend the next hour goofing around at the top of the mountain, putting on a good show in case anyone was watching us. Meanwhile, Asha would be down inside the control center chatting with Ingrid and Mixiplixit. She was going to come out after the hour and hand us a note, then pop back down for the last fifteen minutes to tie up any loose ends.

We made a game out of throwing basketballs off the mountain and seeing where they landed. Jax was the clear winner each time, so he switched gears and gave us some pointers instead. We pretended to hold conversations with Asha is if she was there without a communicator to keep up appearances. Jin was definitely taking advantage of Asha's absence to make a few jokes at her expense. "What's that? Jin was saying. You have to go to the bathroom, Asha?"

"Very funny," Asha said, coming up behind us. "Is this what you do every time my com goes out and I can't hear you?"

I laughed. "Not *all* the time. Just sometimes," I

admitted. "Glad to have you back online." Jin and Jax went back to playing long-range basketball while I went off to chat with Asha. We'd fill them in after the visit, under the cover of the anti-snoring white-noise machine.

Asha smiled and handed me a note. She had transcribed the entire conversation for the past ten minutes. I started to scan it, then realized we would actually have to commit any of the details to memory before heading back up after playground was over. Once again, I cursed the fact that our avatars couldn't bring resources down and we couldn't bring anything back up with us either.

"He seems like a nice, down-to-earth guy," I said to Asha after reading the first page. She rolled her eyes at my bad joke about an alien being down-to-earth. "You know what I mean. There's a lot of information here; what are some of the highlights?" I asked, careful to say as little as possible to attract outside attention.

"Did you see those cars when you were there last?" she asked, trying to keep her words general, too. I realized she meant the purple station wagons that were in the garage down below us. I nodded. I had wondered why there were cars stashed in the middle of a mountain where no one could have driven them in or out. "They can be used as supplies. For transportation. For our friend. You know, the

down-to-earth one. To . . . um . . . lift his spirits."
She mimed sending something up in the air.

It was my turn to roll my eyes. She didn't have
to spell it out for me. Apparently, they were trying
to build something to get our pink friend home, and
those cars had some key pieces they would need. She
flipped the page over, and my eyes widened. It was
a supply list to help build a rocket. Ingrid and the
alien wanted us to help them build a rocket to get
him out of here.

I handed it back to Asha. "No way," I said simply. I wasn't going to be a part of this rebel behavior
anymore. "I'll be there for support and in the interest
of cultural exchange. Safety, for sure. But not an exit
strategy. That's where I draw the line."

Asha shook her head. I wasn't sure if she was out-
right disagreeing with me or if she was telling me to
limit my reaction for now. She took the notes from
me and flipped to another page, then handed it to
me smiling.

"I agree. I just wanted to put it out there," she
said. "Your friend understands, too, and she expected
as much. Here's another list."

This list was much more manageable. It involved
helping them get the supplies they needed to defend
themselves. Between the evil mutant prisoners who
were out for blood and the cadets they were trying to
avoid, they were basically stuck in the tower, cut off

from the rest of the island. Their supplies were running out, and they had no way of getting more without risking exposure. If we could build structures and provide cover, they would be able to venture out and gather the supplies they needed to survive for long enough to build their own rocket *and* get Mixiplixit back home.

"What happens to my friend after that?" I asked.

Ingrid shrugged. "She says she wants to take life one crisis at a time. She said the next crisis will probably come soon enough, and when it did, she'd handle that the way she handled everything else. One day at a time."

That sounded very wise. How could we not help someone with that kind of attitude toward life? I threw caution to the wind and went to the entrance of the lair, about to step inside. It was the least I could do for someone who had given up everything to help someone. Asha held me back, then scribbled a note on the back of one of the papers and handed it to me. "I'll be your messenger. Don't be a fool. You'll risk everything if you go down there and your com goes out."

As much as I wanted to speak with Ingrid in person, I knew Asha was right. Then it hit me. "Ask her to come up here," I wrote.

Asha ducked inside and came back with Ingrid. Using our old sign language, I was able to tell her face-to-face that I would help them survive any way I could, but I couldn't help build the rocket ship. Not yet.

"Where is that rebel spirit?" Ingrid signed back to me.

"I'm trying something new for a while," I said. "I'm going to see how things go if I play by the rules for once." It was my first time admitting my rebellion to another person who came from the same background—I hadn't even told my parents where I was—but it was safe to assume she'd understand after all she had been through. Being a rebel had not only cost Ingrid her freedom. It had turned her into a mutant and had cost her a chance at having a normal life.

"I understand," Ingrid signed back. She gave me a hug. "I know how much you are risking to help us, and I want you to know that we are grateful to you and your friends. More grateful than you will ever know."

A message flashed on my screen, announcing the storm eye was about to close in, and it was headed our way in less than a minute. "It's time for us to go," I signed to her. Ingrid leaned in and gave me a hug. "We will be back soon." I told her.

"Good luck in battle, Rebel!" She signed with a smile. "Fight well."

I returned to my group and signaled we were

done. Jax threw down a long ramp leading off the mountain. I let the others go first, then followed them across it and took a leap into nothingness. As my glider popped out, slowing my freefall, I glanced behind me. Ingrid and the alien were standing at the top of their lair, waving until the storm closed in over them and they disappeared into the mist.

A movement on the map in my visor display caught my eye. "We've got company," Jax announced. I motioned to Ingrid to duck and cover, and then ran to the edge of the cliff to see what was happening. Five avatars were headed our way. They were dressed in SWAT team attire with HQ badges, and they each carried a legendary weapon.

"STEP AWAY FROM THE MOUNTAIN," a voice called into our coms. We each looked at each other, confirming that we had all heard the same announcement. "We are HQMP and we believe you are in extreme danger."

"HQMP?" Asha asked.

"The military police arm of HQ," Jax answered matter of factly. From the way he answered, it sounded like he had run into them before.

"Correct. We are here to protect you," the voice went on as the soldiers continued their approach. The fact that they had heard Asha and Jax's comments meant we wouldn't be able to speak without alerting them to our plans.

"Um, er … Great. Thanks for coming," I replied, trying to stall them so we could make a plan. I motioned to Asha to hand me the paper. We'd have to pass notes in order to communicate. "We had no idea we were in any danger. Jin here was just surveying the land, and we were shooting some hoops to pass the time. Just give us a second to finish up and find our way down." We backed away from their view.

How much do you think they know? I wrote and held the note up to my squad. They all shrugged. I thought for a second and then scribbled another note. *We have to assume they at least know about either Mixy or Ingrid, if not both. Not sure what their weapons can do so we have to be careful.*

Let's draw them away from the mountain, Ingrid wrote. We all nodded in agreement.

"Everything's fine here, officers. Asha's suit is glitching again, but that's about all the excitement we've seen in a while," Jin called into his com.

"We have picked up heat signatures from inside the mountain. We are coming up to investigate," the same voice continued. "Please head to the eye at Tilted Towers where you will be picked up by the drones."

"I thought all life had been wiped out," I replied, trying to keep them talking so we could buy more time. "I thought only avatars can survive here."

"There may be a mutant presence ..." the officer began.

"That's classified information, Major," a woman's voice cut him off.

"They need to understand the danger, Lieutenant," the Major replied. "With all due respect, Ma'am, I was brought here because I'm the expert on the mutant issue. My orders come directly from Sergeant Velasco."

"Mutant issue?" Asha asked, pretending to be surprised and scared. "Are you saying there are mutants down here? Because I saw something really scary leap off the back side of the mountain a while ago and run toward the edge of the island."

"Go check that out, Galahad," the Lieutenant ordered. "And take Melvin with you. Thank you, Asha. I'm glad you understand the urgency of getting you off this mountain as quickly as possible."

I'll alert Ingrid, Asha wrote and headed back into the mouth of the mountain.

"Asha, are you still there?" The Lieutenant called into her com. She sounded nervous.

"She's right here, Ma'am," Jin lied. "Her com is out again."

"Well, stick together," the Major replied. "How did you get up there, anyway?"

I explained that climbing the mountain using our avatars had been part of our training regimen. Then

Jax broke in and suggested they could just build a fort if the climbing was too tough. "We're trained professionals, son, we can handle this," the Lieutenant replied. Jax stifled a laugh. He had counted on her ego getting the better of her. Having them climb up the side of the mountain bought us time to plan. "Meanwhile, I suggest you glide down to safety and head to the eye."

"We'd like to finish our land survey, if you don't mind," Jin broke in. "I'm almost done here."

"You have two minutes to finish up and get out of there," she conceded. We could hear her and the other two officers grunting through their coms. Avatars or not, they clearly were struggling with the climb.

Asha came out into the sunlight and gave us a thumbs up. Then Ingrid appeared behind her. She nodded to me and the others and then walked toward the edge of the cliff where the SWAT team was making their climb. I caught her arm to hold her back. "Don't. They'll see you," I signed to her.

"It's time," she signed back, waiting for me to let go of her arm.

Jin scribbled a quick note and held it up for me to see. *What is she saying? If she goes to the edge, they'll catch her.*

An explosion came from the side of the mountain. We rushed to the edge, but I held Ingrid back with one hand. It was like she was hoping to get caught. One of the officers had tumbled off the rock face from the force of the explosion, and we watched as the drone came to beam up the broken avatar. I looked at Ingrid. "Was it you?" I asked. She smiled and shrugged. *Always the rebel*, I thought.

"Is everyone okay?" The lieutenant called out in a shaky voice.

"We're all fine up here," Asha replied sounding concerned. "I hope no one got hurt."

"Just finish up your survey and get out of there. We don't want any more suits to get damaged in this ridiculous mission," the Lieutenant replied. "That explosion is proof that the mutants are hiding inside the mountain, Ma'am, and they know that we're here. We should head back up to HQ. Sergeant Velasco gave clear orders that once we confirm the mutant presence, we should leave immediately," the Major replied. There was a sense of urgency in his voice. I almost felt bad for the guy. He had clearly spent a lot of time putting together clues and studying the situation only to have the military take over. My first thought was to get angry. It was a typical government move. Then I realized that's what the old rebel me would have thought. The Lieutenant was just doing what she thought was the safe thing, after all.

"We haven't gotten visual confirmation yet," the Lieutenant replied, huffing and puffing her way up the mountain. They had gotten halfway up. I was actually impressed with their climbing skills.

"No sign of any mutants on the ground, Ma'am," Galahad's voice broke in. "We saw the explosion from across the way. Was it a weapon malfunction?"

"We'll have to assume it was a charge coming from inside the mountain," she began, and then seemed to consider Galahad's theory. "It is possible Ron's blaster went off as he was climbing."

"We're heading to your location now," Galahad replied. "We'll take a look at it from the ground."

Ingrid looked disappointed once I signed what we had heard over the coms. She should have been happy that her cover may not have been blown after all. She tried to wrench free from my grasp to peer over the edge, but I held on. "You may be in the clear," I signed. "We can find a way to keep your cover as long as you stay hidden."

She shook her head. "As I said before, it's time. We have a plan," she reassured me. "They don't know how many of us are here. They can't destroy our lair. Not with their avatar weapons. Nothing they can do can hurt us. But now that they know we're here, we don't have to hide." Her hands moved furiously and it was hard for me to keep up with what she was signing. "Now we can start building the ship and all they can do is watch. My question is, now that our secret is out, are you with us?"

She was out of practice, I thought. A good rebel would never blow their cover, and they wouldn't put us at risk. Unless this was her plan all along. She knew they couldn't do anything to her. She was just waiting to be found. Had she been using us all along to lead them to her lair? "You knew." I signed to her. She shrugged again. I looked over at my squad who were all looking at me for answers. I picked up the paper. *You knew this would happen, didn't you?* I repeated the accusation but this time it was on paper so the rest of the squad could join in the conversation.

Ingrid grabbed the paper and wrote back. *We could use this to our advantage.* She looked around at the four of us, searching our faces for some sort of response, but thankfully our avatars were not programmed to have facial expressions. She pulled her arm free again and this time I didn't resist. We stared at each other. She was challenging me to join her or leave her and the alien to fight alone. My squad stood by, watching us both. The dots on my visor were getting closer. The SWAT team was almost there.

"You still have time to duck in there. We can cover for you," I signed. But Ingrid shook her head. Instead, she walked toward the edge of the cliff to await the team's arrival. I looked over at my squad mates who were all waiting patiently, trusting me to do what I felt was right. My rebel heart told me to join Ingrid against the Lieutenant and all she stood for. But my independent heart wasn't sure this was my fight to join.

Ingrid sensed my hesitation. Her eyes were suddenly filled with kindness and compassion. For just a moment, she wasn't a mutant or a rebel. My old friend was back. "Go," she mouthed to me. "I'll be fine." She blew me a kiss and stepped to the edge to await the team's arrival. With one last look at me, she mouthed the words *"Fight well,"* then turned to greet the first climber to arrive.

I returned to my group and signaled we were done. Jax threw down a long ramp leading off the mountain. I let the others go first, then followed them across it and took a leap into nothingness. As my glider popped out, slowing my freefall, I glanced behind me. Ingrid was standing face-to-face with the SWAT team, the storm eye closing in behind her. Soon the team's avatars would be enshrouded in mist and beamed back up. They had run out of time. In the distance over by Tilted Towers, I saw the four drones waiting for our team, the Impossibles. I wasn't sure what kind of reception to expect when we climbed out of our pods, or what we would say when we faced Velasco and the Lieutenant in person, but I was certain that whatever we faced, we would all do it together. And for the time being, that was enough.

ALSO AVAILABLE

ABOUT THE AUTHOR

Cara J. Stevens has written dozens of books for kids, including *Revenge of the Zombie Monks*, an unofficial Minecraft graphic novel. When she's not reading, writing, or hanging out at the beach, she can be found playing pinball and video games. Cara lives in Los Angeles, CA with her husband, two children, and a loud, fluffy dog named Oliver. Visit her online at carajstevens.com.